# A Note from PJ Library®

In this story, Max travels back in time to the days of Jacob and Esau. In the Torah (the first five books of the Bible), these twin grandsons of Abraham and Sarah are archrivals. The story goes that since Esau is born first, he is the rightful recipient of his father's blessing, which gives him certain privileges. Jacob tricks Esau into trading this blessing (for a bowl of lentil soup!). Later, Jacob tricks their father into giving him Esau's blessing by dressing up as Esau. Fearing Esau's anger, Jacob runs away to live with his uncle. Many years later, Jacob journeys home and arranges to meet with Esau. The night before the two brothers meet, Jacob dreams that he is wrestling with an angel. God renames him Israel, which in Hebrew means "one who wrestles with God." (That name, of course, has come to represent the entire Jewish world, all of whom are considered Jacob's descendants.) At the brothers' reunion, Jacob apologizes for what he's done. Esau kindly lets bygones be bygones, as Max sees for himself.

When Max sees Jacob apologize to Esau, he's inspired to do some apologizing of his own. The High Holidays of Rosh Hashanah and Yom Kippur are a perfect time to apologize to people we've hurt over the course of the past year. Centuries ago, the Jewish philosopher Maimonides outlined the ingredients of a good apology: specify what you are sorry for, show that you understand why it's wrong, take full responsibility for the harm you caused, and take steps not to do it again. Everyone makes mistakes, which means that we all have to apologize sometimes. When we make things right with others, we are returning to the best version of ourselves. That's why we refer to this process as teshuva, which in Hebrew means "returning." To learn more about teshuva and the High Holidays, visit **pjlibrary.org/highholidays**.

# A Note from PJ Library®

## Talk It Over

How are Max and Jacob alike? How are they different?

Do you know any siblings who sometimes fight? What are those fights about?

What lessons about apologizing does Max learn from Jacob?

Has a friend ever apologized to you? What happened? How do you think the friend felt—and how did you feel?

Can you think of someone to whom you'd like to apologize? What would you say?

## About PJ Library

The gift of PJ Library is made possible by thousands of generous supporters, your Jewish community, the PJ Library Alliance, and the Harold Grinspoon Foundation. PJ Library shares Jewish culture and values through quality children's books that reflect the diversity of Jewish customs and practice. To learn more about the program and ways to connect to local activities, visit **pjlibrary.org.**

# TORAH TIME TRAVEL

## Max and the Not-So-Perfect Apology

by Carl Harris Shuman

illustrated by Rory Walker
and Michael Garton

For my parents, Reba and Bernie Shuman (*z"l*) — C.H.S.

*A midrash is a creative retelling of a Torah story. Rooted in love for the story itself, a good midrash helps us reimagine biblical characters and explore what we can learn from them. This book is a midrash that expands on the story of the reunion between Jacob and Esau at the Jabbok River, many, many years after Jacob stole Esau's blessing of the firstborn. It is one of the Torah's central stories of forgiveness and teaches us that we are all meant to wrestle with the hard question of how best to make someone whole whom we may have wronged.*

Apples & Honey Press, An Imprint of Behrman House Publishers
Millburn, New Jersey 07041
www.applesandhoneypress.com

Text copyright © 2024 by Carl Harris Shuman. Illustrations copyright © 2024 by Behrman House
ISBN 978-1-68115-615-6

Library of Congress Cataloging-in-Publication Data
Names: Shuman, Carl Harris, author. | Walker, Rory, illustrator. | Garton, Michael, illustrator.
Title: Max and the not-so-perfect apology / by Carl Harris Shuman ;
   illustrated by Rory Walker and Michael Garton.
Description: Millburn, New Jersey : Apples & Honey Press, 2024. | Series:
   Torah time travel | Audience: Ages 6-8. | Audience: Grades 2-3. |
   Summary: Max wants to travel back to find out what really happened
   between the biblical brothers Jacob and Esau, but Emma is too busy with
   her new friend Eitan to go on an adventure with Max.
Identifiers: LCCN 2023031491 | ISBN 9781681156156 (hardcover)
Subjects: LCSH: Bible. Old Testament--History of Biblical events--Fiction.
   | CYAC: Bible. Old Testament--History of Biblical events--Fiction. |
   Time travel--Fiction. | Friendship--Fiction. | Jews--Fiction.
Classification: LCC PZ7.1.S51813 Mav 2024 | DDC [Fic]--dc23

Design by Susan and David Neuhaus/NeuStudio. Edited by Leslie Kimmelman
Printed in China

9 8 7 6 5 4 3 2 1

0724/B2545/A7

# Chapter 1

# A Frantic Beginning

**A**s soon as the morning sun landed on his face Max jumped out of bed. Unfortunately, when he stepped down, he stubbed his big toe on his latest invention, a cardboard time machine sitting next to his nightstand.

"Ouch!" he shouted.

"Gesundheit," Miri replied. Resting on the time machine's dashboard, Miri was a smartphone that Max had reprogrammed to help him travel through time.

Already late, Max washed only the left side of his face, brushed his upper but not lower teeth, skipped the top two buttons on his shirt, tied his left light-up sneaker, and ate only one of three pancakes at breakfast. Max's mom hovered over him with a glass of milk. Max bolted from his chair. "Sorry! No time! Big day at school! Gotta go!" He blew his mom a kiss and sped out the front door.

Once outside, Max stopped and slapped his forehead. "The shoebox!"

Max ran back inside, clambered up the stairs, raced into his bedroom, dove under his bed, and tossed out

underwear and several gizmos and gadgets. "Miri, can you help me find my diorama?"

"Maternal units do not live under beds."

Max rolled his eyes. "Not *my mama. Diorama.* Emma and I are building a *diorama* for Mrs. Mooshky's Torah class. We're going to show how Jacob pretended to be his older twin brother, Esau, so that Isaac, their blind father, would mistake Jacob for Esau and give him Esau's super-duper older brother blessing. I'm in charge of the shoebox. Emma's bringing Jacob, Esau, and Isaac."

"Three humans cannot fit in a shoebox," Miri replied.

"Jacob, Esau, and Isaac lived thousands of years ago! Emma's bringing dolls, not real people."

Max kept searching for the shoebox. A map of Max's room appeared on Miri's screen. "Redirecting. Proceed to the route."

"Aha!" Max raced toward his drafting table and spied his shoebox under a pile of diagrams. He grinned, grabbed the box, and headed for the stairs.

"Wish me luck!" he shouted over his shoulder. "Mrs. Mooshky said the team with the best diorama wins a prize!"

Max flew out the front door and looked for Emma, his best friend. While he waited, Eitan whizzed by on his two-wheeler. Unlike Max, Eitan knew how to ride a bike without training wheels and how to climb the jungle gym. Max sighed; sometimes he wished he could be more like Eitan.

Suddenly Max felt a tap on his shoulder. "Hey, co-pilot!"

Max spun around. "Emma!" As usual, Emma was all in pink.

Max proudly showed Emma his shoebox. "I stayed

up late to cut out all these doors and windows."

Emma opened one of the tiny windows. "What a clever idea! Ventilation is *so* important in the desert."

Max wiped his brow with his sleeve. "Yeah, when we crossed the Red Sea with Moses it was so hot I almost fainted."

"Kelev and I talk all the time about taking another trip in your time machine!" Emma exclaimed.

Max raised an eyebrow. "Umm . . . Kelev is a poodle."

"So what's your point?" Emma replied, showing him the contents of her pink backpack as they raced to school.

Max peered inside. "Did you bring them?"

Emma pulled out three short, pudgy dolls. "Ta-da!"

Max raised both eyebrows. "Trolls?"

"Aren't they cute?" Emma replied. "I thought of using my Ken dolls—but they're too big for one shoebox."

"But . . . but . . . the trolls are naked!" Max exclaimed.

"No problem! Emma fished some felt sheets from her backpack and waved them in the air. "See? We can make little troll tunics and matching *kippot*."

Max placed one of the trolls in his shoebox. "He fits! Unfortunately . . . he also has pink hair."

Emma's eyes twinkled. "Yes, isn't it sublime? I like thinking outside the box!"

"What kind of prize do you think we'll get?" Max asked. "I'm hoping for a year's free subscription to *Cardboard Inventions*."

Emma stuffed the felt sheets and two trolls into her backpack. "Pink zirconia jewelry might be nice. Or maybe a six-month supply of tuna sandwiches."

Max heard the school's warning bell. As he and Emma ran past the bike racks, Max saw Eitan remove a glittery cardboard tent from his two-wheeler's basket. Max gulped. His hands began to sweat. Maybe winning the prize for best diorama wasn't going to be as easy as he'd imagined.

# Chapter 2

# **Upsetting the Apple Cart**

**M**ax's heart sank as soon as he entered Mrs. Mooshky's classroom. The desks had been rearranged. Instead of sitting next to Emma, Max was seated next to Sophie and Wendy. Emma was nearby, next to Eitan and Henry.

"Good morning," Mrs. Mooshky said. "As you see, I've changed your seating assignments so that you can work on your dioramas in groups of three instead of two."

Wendy nervously pulled on a blond pigtail. "Did we do something wrong?"

Mrs. Mooshky chuckled. "Oh, no, dear. I just like upsetting the apple cart occasionally. Learning to adapt to change is important. Plus, now you'll get to know more of your classmates."

Max slunk in his seat. He felt the "best diorama" prize slipping through his fingers; Sophie's clay figurines resembled space aliens rather than people, and he couldn't help rolling his eyes at Wendy's dorky mini plastic furniture.

Emma suddenly jumped up. "Mrs. Mooshky, I liked the apple cart the way it was!"

Mrs. Mooshky scanned the three desks belonging to Emma's team. "Eitan has built quite an impressive cardboard tent. Why don't you give your new partners a chance?"

Emma hesitated—and handed Eitan her two trolls. Eitan gave Emma a high five. "These are way cool. Thanks, partner!"

Max's head began to throb.

Henry reached into his knapsack for a bag filled with sand.

Emma spread Henry's sand on the tent floor. "Very authentic!" she exclaimed.

Henry beamed. "It's from the beach."

Eitan then leaned over and whispered in Emma's ear. Emma tiptoed over to Max. "I'm sorry, Max, but we need that third troll."

Max reluctantly handed Emma the troll. He then watched Sophie try to fit her clay aliens on Wendy's plastic furniture, only to see everything topple over. Max put his head on his desk and groaned.

"Max, what's wrong?" Mrs. Mooshky asked.

Max looked up and glared at Eitan. "I think I know how Esau felt when Jacob stole his blessing. As far as I'm concerned, Jacob was the bad guy in this story."

"Uh-oh," Wendy muttered.

"Jacob's supposed to be one of our heroes," Sophie whispered.

Mrs. Mooshky raised an eyebrow. "What do you mean, Max?"

Max stammered. "Well, J-J-Jacob tricked Isaac into thinking that he was Esau and then stole his brother's blessing. Doesn't that make him the bad guy?"

Mrs. Mooshky jabbed the air with her finger. "Actually, Max, you're not completely off the mark! Jacob *was* dishonest. In fact, Esau was so mad he wanted to kill him! So Jacob fled Canaan and didn't return for more than *twenty years*!"

Max imagined that if more than twenty years was the price for stealing a blessing, Eitan should get thirty years for trying to steal Emma's friendship *and* the prize for best diorama. Why did Mrs. Mooshky have to mess things up?

"When Jacob finally returned to Canaan, *did* Esau kill him?" Wendy asked.

Mrs. Mooshky rubbed her hands together. There was a gleam in her eye. "Not exactly . . ."

Henry pulled at his bow tie. "Not *exactly*?"

Mrs. Mooshky spoke in a hush. "Well, some rabbis believe that Esau never truly forgave Jacob for stealing his special blessing and—instead of kissing Jacob when they met twenty years later near the Jabbok River—*bit him in the neck.*"

"No way!" Max exclaimed.

"Esau was a vampire?" Eitan asked. "*Way cool!*"

Wendy twirled her pigtails. "They say Esau was *very* hairy. Maybe he was a werewolf!"

Was Esau a vampire? A werewolf? Max was ready for another time travel adventure to find out. He hoped that Emma still wanted to be his co-pilot. After all, Eitan may have had a glittery tent—but Max had a time machine!

# Chapter 3

## Scaredy Pants

**W**hen Max reached the playground at recess, Emma was already atop the jungle gym. Looking up, Max gripped the first rung but, afraid of heights, let go when his heart started to race.

"Maybe you could come down?" he pleaded.

"Oh, come on, Max," Emma replied, "what's the worst that can happen?"

"I could slip, fall, hit my head, and watch my brains fall out."

"So don't climb to the top! We've traveled thousands of years in your time machine. How's that safer?"

Max looked around. "*Shh*! It's a secret! Anyway, I built the *you-know-what* out of very sturdy cardboard, using only quality parts."

"Sorry about the third troll," Emma told him. "We needed it for our diorama and Eitan was being—"

"A nincompoop," Max mumbled.

"A what?" Emma shouted.

Max kicked the jungle gym. "A NINCOMPOOP!"

Just then, Eitan raced across the playground, scampered to the highest rung, and grabbed at Emma's floppy hat. Emma giggled.

Unsure if Eitan heard him, Max shook his head and muttered, "I guess this isn't the best time to ask Emma if she wants to go on another adventure."

Max spied Sophie and Wendy on the swings and walked over to them.

"Hey, Max," Wendy said. "Wanna do corkscrews with us?"

"It's exhilarating!" Sophie said.

"Exhila-what?" Wendy asked.

"From the Latin *hilarus*, 'to make cheerful,'" Sophie explained.

Max hopped on the empty seat next to Sophie. "What's the Latin for 'losing your closest friend'?"

"Who are we talking about?" Wendy asked.

Max pointed to Emma, who was scooting across the jungle gym with Eitan.

"Looks like Mrs. Mooshky's plan is working," Wendy said.

Max's shoulders slumped.

"Why don't you invite them to do corkscrews with us?" Sophie asked.

Max twisted the swing's chains. Eitan built a glittery tent. *Clink clink clink clink.* Emma's team was probably going to win the prize. *Clink clink clink.* It had taken Max such a long time to find a good friend like Emma. *Clink clink.* And now Emma was playing with Eitan the Nincompoop. *Clink.*

Suddenly the tightly twisted chains unraveled—*clink-clink-clink-clink-clink*—and sent Max twirling in the opposite direction.

"Wheeeeeee!" Wendy shouted, twirling to the right.

"Stupendous!" Sophie exclaimed, twirling to the left.

"Ugh," Max muttered, nauseated as he watched Emma and Eitan chase each other around the playground.

"You're it!" Eitan yelled, zigging.

"No, *you're* it!" Emma replied, zagging.

Eitan raced ahead. Emma stopped to catch her breath.

"Now's your chance!" Sophie said.

"Huh?" Max asked.

Wendy cocked her head in Emma's direction.

Max jumped off his swing and ran to Emma. "Wait up!"

Max remembered the first time he'd asked Emma to go time traveling and, like then, scrunched his eyes closed. "Wanna come for Sunday brunch? We're having challah French toast. Afterward we could visit Canaan to see if Esau was a vampire!"

Max opened his eyes. Emma was staring at her pink sneakers. "Umm, well you see, umm . . ."

Max was shocked. "What? You don't want to go?"

"It's not that I don't *want* to," Emma replied. "It's just that—well, Eitan invited Henry and me to ride bikes on Sunday. I'm sorry."

Max stomped his left light-up sneaker. So Eitan had stolen his best friend after all!

"Fine!" he shouted. "Be that way! At least our diorama won't have stupid naked trolls with pink hair!"

"I thought you liked the trolls!" Emma exclaimed.

"I lied! They're stupid! Just like you!" Max replied.

Emma stomped her sneakers. "Fine! At least I won't have to time travel with a scaredy pants!"

Max trudged back to the swings.

"So?" Sophie asked.

"She said I'm a scaredy pants," Max replied. "I am not! I'm just very careful. Anyway, what's the big deal? All I did was call her stupid."

Sophie just raised an eyebrow.

# Chapter 4

# Max Goes It Alone

**O**n Sunday, Max slumped at the breakfast table, picking at his French toast. His mom was sipping coffee. His dad was doing a crossword puzzle and grimacing.

"Seeing Emma today?" his mom asked.

Max hid behind his *Cardboard Inventions* magazine. "No, she has other plans," he muttered.

Max's dad frowned. "Don't mumble."

"I SAID SHE HAS OTHER PLANS!!"

Max's parents glanced at each other. "Want to talk about it?" his mom asked.

"No!"

His dad put the puzzle aside. "Want to go biking? We could practice riding without training wheels."

Perfect, Max thought, more humiliation! What if Emma and Eitan were riding their bikes and saw him fall? "Thanks, but I think I'll go to my room and invent something. May I be excused?"

Before his parents could answer, Max grabbed a bag of popcorn from the pantry and ran upstairs. Then he changed into his Power Patrol suit, his X-ray goggles, and his new cape, which was also his mom's striped tablecloth.

Max crawled into his time machine, marveling at the handiwork he'd cobbled together from a large cardboard box, a drone dashboard, tricycle handlebars, and an Erector Set motor. Since his Exodus from Egypt with Emma, he'd added an exhaust system, courtesy of his mother's old window fan, and a convertible roof, courtesy of his father's broken umbrella.

"Miri, I need to travel back in time to see if Esau really bit Jacob."

"To avoid landing in the Middle Ages, I must calculate the body mass-to-time ratio. Any other passengers?" Miri asked.

"Nope," Max said glumly. "But maybe I'll find some new friends there."

Max pressed the orange ignition button. The Erector Set motor purred, the dashboard lights blinked, and Max's room began to spin. Max, hurtling through time, found the flight even more nauseating than corkscrews on the playground, and he prayed for the French toast to stay in his stomach.

Eventually the spinning slowed, and a different,

greener world came into view. Once his machine
shuddered to a halt, Max peered out the window.
Slivers of yellow and pink light were just emerging
over the horizon. A river tumbled over sun-bleached
rocks.

Once he got his bearings, Max wobbled out of the
machine and into the backside of a smelly, speckled
lamb.

"Baa-aa."

Max clambered back into his machine. "Yuck!"

"Wooly ruminants can see behind them without turning their heads," Miri said.

"Which means . . . ?"

"I believe the lamb just said hello," Miri replied. "Why don't you introduce yourself?"

Max crawled out of his machine again and placed some popcorn kernels on the ground. The lamb devoured them and licked Max's face. After hiding the time machine behind a tree and muting Miri, Max began walking. The lamb followed, prancing across the field and occasionally circling back for more popcorn.

"I think I'll call you *Chaver*," Max said. "It's Hebrew for 'friend.'"

"Baa-aa."

Max reached out to scratch Chaver's head, but the lamb suddenly bolted across the meadow. Max chased Chaver and soon spotted a boy who was ordering the trees to bow down to him. Frightened but also intrigued, Max crouched in the tall grass to watch. Chaver bleated.

"Shh!" Max said.

The boy turned around. "Who's there?"

Max slowly emerged from the grass.

The boy's jaw dropped as he scanned Max from head to toe. "You're the strangest thing I've ever seen!"

"*I'm* strange? *You* were talking to trees!" Max replied.

"Fair enough," the boy said.

Chaver bleated and circled Max's legs. The boy looked suspiciously at Max. "What are you doing with one of our lambs?"

"He's yours? I kind of adopted him."

"Well, you can't have him. I own him! "

The boy pointed to the bag of popcorn in Max's hand. "But . . . maybe I'll let you borrow him in exchange for whatever that is."

"It's popcorn." Max handed him the bag.

The boy tore it open and started munching. "Mmm . . . good." He emptied the bag into his mouth, handed it back to Max, and burped. "I'm Joey. Me and my pop, Jacob, own everything you see, and I'm his favorite."

Max felt his spine tingle. So this was Joseph! Mrs. Mooshky's class hadn't studied him yet, but Max knew from Junior Congregation that Joseph was Jacob's son. Max also recalled that Joseph had weird dreams about bowing wheat stalks and stars, got thrown into a pit because his brothers found him obnoxious, became a slave, moved to Egypt, and became something like its vice president. Max had no difficulty believing the obnoxious part.

Max gazed at the surrounding fields and trees. "Where are we?"

"We're near the Jabbok River, nincompoop," Joey replied. "We're supposed to be meeting my uncle Esau any day now. He and Pop had a blow-up back in the day. We're here to see if Uncle Esau's still holding a grudge."

Ouch! Max had never been called a nincompoop before.

Joey stared at Max. "Your clothes are weird. Are you an Ishmaelite?"

"Druid," Max replied.

"Never heard of them," Joey said. "What's your name?"

"Max."

A breeze made Max's cape billow.

"Cool wings, Max," Joey said. "Can I have them?"

"No," Max replied.

Joey stomped his foot. "*What do you mean I can't have them? I always—*"

"Oy! What's the problem?"

Max looked up. A disheveled man with a straggly beard was limping toward them. He looked as if he hadn't slept all night. Joey ran to him.

"Pop, this Druid won't give me his wings!" Joey whined.

Max felt another tingling sensation. Jacob? He didn't look anything like the trickster that Mrs. Mooshky described! This Jacob had kind eyes and a gentle voice.

Jacob looked warily at Max. "Are you an angel?"

"No, I'm just a kid. And they're not wings. It's a cape."

"So, cape boy, do you have a name?" Jacob asked.

"His name's Max," Joey replied.

"Max, would you trade me your cape for a spotted goat?"

"I can't. I borrowed the cape from my mom," Max replied.

Jacob grinned. "How about two spotted goats?"

Max shook his head.

"*But Pop*—," Joey whined.

"Joey, Max said no. If we get back to Canaan, I'll make you a coat."

"Like that one—but with more colors?" Joey asked.

"Sure," Jacob replied, "whatever you want."

Jacob doubled over in pain. "Ow!"

"Pop!" Joey exclaimed. "Are you okay?"

Jacob winced. "It's my hip. It's a long story . . . but a really good one. I'll explain once you boys help me to that boulder over there. I can barely stand."

Uh-oh, thought Max. If Jacob can't stand, how can he walk? If he can't walk, how can he meet Esau? And if he doesn't meet Esau, how am I going to find out if Esau is a vampire?

# Chapter 5

# A Mysterious Angel

Joey and Max helped Jacob hobble to the nearest boulder. Behind them, Jacob's camp was beginning to stir; the women were busy drawing water from the river, and Joey's older brothers were chasing lambs and goats across the surrounding hills.

Max stood beside the boulder, next to Chaver. "So how'd you get hurt?"

Jacob rubbed his hip. "I ran into an angel."

"Cool!" Joey exclaimed, as he joined Max and

Chaver. "What did he look like?"

"Actually, a little like me," Jacob answered. "Gray beard. Maybe a bit overweight."

"Did he strike your hip with a lightning bolt?" Max asked.

"No, he wrestled me to the ground and wrenched my hip from its socket."

"Eww!" Max and Joey exclaimed.

"And, after I insisted on a blessing, he gave me a new name."

"The Avenger?" Joey asked.

"Stone Cold Jacob?" Max asked.

"Israel," Jacob replied. "It means 'wrestling with God.'"

The boys' eyes widened. "You wrestled with *God*?"

"Technically, God's angel," Jacob replied. "Or maybe my own conscience."

"Your conscience?" Max asked.

Jacob glumly placed his head in his hands. "I did some terrible things to my older brother when we were growing up. First, I tricked him out of his birthright— his rightful inheritance—for a bowl of lentils. Then I tricked my father into believing that I was Esau and stole my brother's special blessing meant for the firstborn. At the time, I told myself, 'What's the big deal?' Now that I am older I understand how Esau must have felt and want to make amends."

*"What's the big deal?"* Max had said the exact same thing after he insulted Emma. It didn't sound any better coming from Jacob.

"Have you apologized to Uncle Esau yet?" Joey asked.

"I sent him a bunch of our best animals—but frankly, I'm not sure that's enough."

Jacob looked at Max. "Have *you* ever done something wrong and felt guilty about it?"

Max, red-faced, paused and whispered, "I recently called someone a nincompoop."

"So?" Joey replied. "I call everybody a nincompoop. Especially my stupid brothers."

Jacob placed a finger over his mouth. "Shh, let Max continue."

Max lowered his eyes. "I also said some really mean things to my best friend."

Jacob beckoned for Max to join him on the rock. "So what happened?"

Max sat next to Jacob. "Nothing yet. I'm not sure what to say or do."

Jacob gave Max a small hug. "We seem to be in the same boat. Maybe we can help each other figure it out."

Suddenly Joey heard a rumbling sound in the 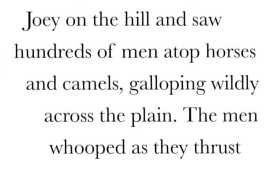 distance and pointed. Max joined Joey on the hill and saw hundreds of men atop horses and camels, galloping wildly across the plain. The men whooped as they thrust

spears into the air. A man with a tangle of coppery, greasy hair led the charge. When the leader gave the signal for his men to stop, Max and Joey ran back to Jacob and Chaver.

"I think it's your brother!" Max said breathlessly.

Jacob trembled.

"Come on, Pop," Joey urged. "Max and I will help you up the hill."

At the crest, Jacob peered at the crowd in front of him. "Who comes to say 'I forgive you' with an army? Quick, run to the camp and warn the family!"

Max and Joey ran back and scurried from tent to tent.

"Take cover!" they shouted.

"Esau and his army are coming! And they have spears!"

After everyone took cover, Max and Joey ran back to Jacob, who was nervously limping back and forth.

"Maybe the angel wrenched your hip so that Esau will feel sorry for you and forgive you for stealing his blessing," Max said.

Jacob stroked his beard. "From your lips to God's ears!"

Joey tugged at his father's robe. "Pop, to show how sorry you truly are, why don't you bow down before Uncle Esau?"

"Bow down? With this hip?"

"Last night, I had this weird dream about a lamb bowing to a goat seven times and—"

Suddenly Esau dismounted and pointed to his brother on the hill. "*Jacob!*"

Jacob shuddered. "*Here I am!*"

Max and Joey helped Jacob descend the slope. Jacob limped across the field and began to bow down. But when he tried to get up, he stumbled and fell.

Esau ran toward Jacob. "Brother! *I'm coming for you!*"

Max's heart raced. Was Esau running to help Jacob off the ground—or finish him off?

Jacob looked back at Joey and Max. "Help me!"

Joey, Max, and Chaver rushed toward Jacob. Joey and Max bent down and helped Jacob to his feet.

Jacob took a step, but his legs buckled again. Esau lurched toward Jacob. Max and Joey jumped back. Max closed his eyes. Then Jacob said, "Ow!"

Was Esau biting Jacob in the neck? Or worse?

# Chapter 6

# Water Under the Bridge

**W**hen Max opened his eyes, Jacob and Esau were crying in each other's arms. Max didn't see any blood or bite marks on Jacob's neck. "I guess Esau's human after all," Max grumbled, disappointed that he wouldn't get to see his first vampire.

Clearly bored by the wailing, Joey tugged on his father's sleeve. "Hey, Pop, aren't you gonna introduce us?"

Jacob wiped his nose on his sleeve, puffed out his chest, and beckoned for his family to come forward.

"These are my wives and kids. And this is Joey, the apple of my eye!"

Esau looked at Max. "And what's he? A potato?"

"Druid," Joey answered.

Max pointed to the hills. "From the north."

"Lebanon?" Esau asked

Max grinned. "Even farther."

Esau scanned the encampment. "And all of this?"

"God has favored me with these tents, animals, and servants," Jacob replied.

Esau winced. Jacob smacked his forehead. "Oy! I keep sticking my sandal in my mouth. How can I make it up to you? You want another goat? How about a camel? God knows, I have more than my fair share."

This time, Esau rolled his eyes.

"Okay, nix the goats and camels." Jacob looked at Chaver, but Max quickly threw his arms around the small lamb.

Jacob then frantically pushed a donkey forward. "How about this?"

Esau pushed the donkey back.

Max frowned. Clearly Esau was still carrying many years' worth of hurt on his back. Just as clearly, Jacob was still wrestling to find the right apology to salve his brother's wounds. Wrestling!

That was it! Max tugged on Jacob's sleeve. "When you wrestled with the angel, you insisted on a blessing . . ."

Jacob's eyes widened. "The blessing! Of course!" he exclaimed. "I'll be right back. Joey, come into the tent with me."

Outside, Max and Chaver sat on the grass while Esau paced. "What are they doing in there? The last time my brother disappeared into a tent, I lost my place in the world."

Esau sat next to Max. "So what's your story?"

"I'm fleeing a bad situation," Max replied.

Esau scratched Chaver's fluffy head. "You stole someone's blessing?"

"No. I called one person a nincompoop and my best friend stupid."

Esau placed Chaver in his lap. "Did you apologize?"

Max shook his head. "I'm not even sure one of them heard me. Do I have to apologize if the person doesn't know about the insult?"

Esau raised an eyebrow. "I think you know the answer. Anything else?"

Before Max could reply, Joey emerged from the tent and handed his uncle a small scroll. "Uncle Esau, Pop wanted me to write these words down to give to you. He said you'd understand."

Jacob studied his brother from the tent's entrance.

Esau read slowly from the scroll. "*Blessed . . . are . . . they . . . who . . . bless . . . you.*"

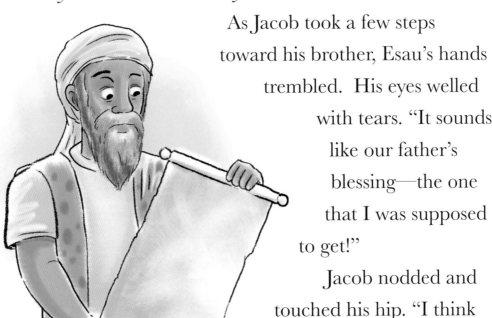

As Jacob took a few steps toward his brother, Esau's hands trembled. His eyes welled with tears. "It sounds like our father's blessing—the one that I was supposed to get!"

Jacob nodded and touched his hip. "I think

that when I stole your blessing, I stole a piece of myself
as well. Until now, I didn't understand that to make
myself whole, I had to make you whole again, too."

As the setting sun fringed the clouds with wisps
of pink light, Max watched Jacob and
Esau walk arm-in-arm toward the
Jabbok River. He was beginning
to understand how a good
apology worked—so he was
startled when he saw Esau
gather his men and hug his
brother goodbye.

With Chaver in tow,
Max and Joey ran to the river's
edge. Max tugged on Esau's
tunic. "I don't get it."

"Yeah, Pop," Joey added,
"I thought you guys made up! Why is Uncle Esau
leaving?"

Jacob placed his hands on the boys' shoulders. "I'm blessed that Esau accepted my apology. Although he offered to travel with us, I decided that there's still too much hurt between us. It's probably best to go our separate ways and stay on good terms by keeping our distance."

Esau ruffled Jacob's hair. "Yeah, too much water under the bridge."

Max and Joey looked at the river. "What bridge?"

Jacob chuckled. "It's an expression. It means that too much time has gone by to make everything right."

Max looked back across the field to the grove of trees where he had hidden his time machine. Whether it was two days or four thousand years since he last saw Emma, Max was afraid that if he didn't soon return and apologize, the bridge to his friendship with Emma might wash away in a flood of resentment. "I gotta go home!" he blurted out.

Jacob hugged Max. "May you find peace."

Esau gently pulled the X-ray goggles over Max's eyes. "In case you should run into any sandstorms."

Joey grabbed Chaver. "If I give you the lamb, will you stay?"

Chaver wriggled in Joey's arms.

Max considered the offer for a moment. Then he shook his head. Chaver was his friend, but he needed a co-pilot who could say more than "baa-aa."

# Chapter 7

# Climbing to the Top Rung

The sun was setting when Max departed. As he and Miri traveled through time, Max was surprised that he didn't feel the urge to throw up. This was the smoothest ride yet—until the time machine landed next to his bed, let out a puff of smoke, shuddered, and died.

"*Beeeep! Beeeep! This is the emergency broadcast system!*" Miri screeched.

Max jumped out of the machine, dove under his

bed, and emerged with a fire extinguisher. "What is it, Miri?"

"The machine's exhaust system just went *kaput.*"

Max grabbed his Mr. Fixit toolkit and crawled under the time machine. The blade on his mother's old fan was no longer spinning. It had been a long day and Max was exhausted. "I'll try to fix this after school tomorrow. I'm going to bed."

While asleep, Max dreamt that he couldn't repair his time machine, that Eitan had built a faster and sleeker model from the school's jungle gym, and that Eitan and Emma were planning their own Torah trip—without him. Max awoke groggy, sweating, and anxious.

"It's about time!" Miri exclaimed. "You slept over!"

"I think you mean *overslept.*"

To make up for lost time, Max jumped out of bed, quickly washed the right side of his face, brushed his lower teeth, tied his right light-up sneaker, and ate one of two French toast slices at breakfast. "Sorry! Gotta go!" he said to his mother, bolting. "I have something important to tell Emma before school starts. Bye!"

Max raced outside as Emma, Eitan, and Henry zoomed by on their bikes.

Max jumped up and down. "Wait!!"

No one stopped—or even acknowledged him. "Maybe they didn't hear me," Max mumbled as he ran to catch up. Unfortunately, by the time he arrived at school, the late bell was ringing and Max raced into class alone.

Sophie and Wendy were already redecorating the diorama. Sophie's clay figurines now looked more like human beings, and Wendy's furniture was now made of several well-crafted popsicle stick pieces. Max fingered their handiwork. "Wow! These are great! We might win the prize for best diorama after all!"

Sophie pulled a tube of glitter glue from her bookbag and began to apply it to the shoebox.

"Maybe. But you still hurt our feelings on Friday when you made faces at our work."

Max was about to point out that the faces he made on Friday resulted in a better diorama on Monday, but he decided he'd rather have friends than be right. "I'm sorry," he said.

"Apology accepted," Sophie and Wendy chirped. Maybe having Sophie and Wendy as diorama partners wasn't so bad after all, Max thought. And maybe having new friends was even better.

After morning class, the recess bell rang. When he made it to the playground, Max spied Emma and Eitan atop the jungle gym. Eitan was trying to steal Emma's hat again and Emma was giggling. "This is hopeless," Max muttered. "I might as well look for another best friend."

Then Max thought about all the ways Jacob had tried to say "I'm sorry" and what had finally worked. Max gritted his teeth.

He climbed the first rung of the jungle gym. *An apology comes from the heart.*

He climbed the second rung. *An apology is simple and direct.*

He climbed to the top rung. *An apology doesn't involve making lame excuses for bad behavior. And it doesn't require donkeys and camels!*

Max grinned. Without realizing it, he had just conquered his fear of heights and was now a gazillion feet off the ground.

Eitan scampered over to Max. "Hey, Max-O, let's chase Emma!"

Max blushed. "Eitan, I'm sorry I called you a nincompoop on Friday."

Eitan sat on the top bar. "You did? Why?"

Max hesitated before answering. "I was jealous."

"Of me?"

Max gingerly inched his way over to Eitan and sat down next to him. "Well, of your amazing tent."

"Your diorama is way cool, too," Eitan replied. "I especially like all the windows and doors."

Max sat up tall. "You noticed? I stayed up late to make them."

Max looked at Emma, who was playing at the far end of the jungle gym. "I also called you a nincompoop because Emma is my best friend, and I was afraid she was beginning to like you more—"

Emma scampered over and plopped herself down on the bar, facing Eitan and Max. "Remember me?"

Max looked directly at Emma and blushed. "I'm sorry I called you stupid. You were right to keep your promise to Eitan to ride bikes with him."

Emma adjusted her floppy hat but said nothing.

Eitan gently poked Emma. "I think you're supposed to say, 'Apology accepted.'"

Emma hopped to the rung below. Eitan followed. "Let me think about it," she said.

Max's heart beat faster. Was this the end of their friendship?

Emma jumped to the lowest rung. Then she looked up at Max and squinted at him for several seconds. Finally she rolled her eyes. "Okay. Apology accepted. And sorry I called you a scaredy pants."

Max looked down to see the playground spinning below. "Scaredy pants? Me?" he replied, his voice quavering.

Eitan reached up. "Here, take my arm."

Together, Max and Eitan descended until they reached Emma. All three then hopped off and ran to the swings.

"You know, Max," Eitan said, "there's no law that says you have to have just *one* best friend."

"Maybe having a couple is better," Emma said.

Max twisted his seat to face Eitan. "Now that we're friends, can I ask you a question?"

"Sure."

"You're a good builder. Know anything about fixing fans?"

Eitan sat upright. "I can fix almost anything. I have a Mr. Fixit toolkit!"

Max twisted his swing another notch. "Me too! Wanna come over this afternoon with Emma?"

Emma twisted her seat to face Max and Eitan. "Sounds like a plan. I'll bring my hammer—and some pink lemonade."

Emma and Max looked at each other. Maybe it was time for a new adventure. And maybe—just maybe— it was time for another co-pilot.

# A Note for Families

**A**pologies are mysterious things, sometimes difficult to make and sometimes difficult to accept.

Just ask Max. Jealous of Emma's budding friendship with Eitan, Max calls Emma "stupid" and Eitan a "nincompoop." Unsure of how best to apologize to them, Max travels back in time to witness one of the Torah's most important stories about forgiveness. There, he learns firsthand from two biblical brothers. He sees how hard it is for Jacob to right a decades-old wrong against his brother Esau and what it takes to make both of them whole again.

For some people, unlocking the mystery of how to say "I'm sorry" from the heart is like wrestling with an angel. For other people, it is like climbing to the top of a very tall jungle gym.

Have you ever been jealous and, because of it, hurt someone's feelings? What did you do to make things right? Has anyone ever hurt your feelings? Did you accept that person's apology? Is it sometimes okay to forgive but then part ways?

How have you learned to unlock the mystery of forgiveness?